For Marjorie —
All my best wishes,
Marc
9.3.94

# MOVING DAYS

Marc Harshman

ILLUSTRATED BY

Wendy Popp

COBBLEHILL BOOKS · DUTTON/NEW YORK

A snake's skin, white, and light as air! Tangled in old socks and rags, I found it under the rocking chair in the shed. Dad smiled and said he was glad I'd found only that.

A month ago Mom and Dad told me we were moving. I'd said, "Sure, that's OK," but it wasn't really. Not only were we moving; we were moving far away, and to a town. No more woods across the road, no more Jimmy Tolson just down the road. But today there was this great snake's skin. I tried to forget the rest.

"Who's in these pictures, Mom?" I asked as I helped her clean out a closet later. "They all look like rock 'n' roll stars."

"Believe it or not, those are our friends from college and your mom and dad are in some of those shots."

"No, come on, Mom," and then she pointed to one snapshot of three girls with long hair and long dresses. Sure enough, looking closer, I could see her, my mom, twenty years ago, smiling pretty, and as she said, "ready to change the world." I put that one back carefully. When I turned around, Mom was laughing.

"Oh, this is too good, Tommy! Come here, come here!" she demanded, giggling, "come and look at your dashing father!"

It was funny—Mom laughing so hard that she got me laughing. And it was strange because Dad's almost bald now, and there he stood with hair falling over his shoulders. I'm not sure about dashing, but he did look cool. It was all I could think of the rest of the day.

I dreamed about them that night—father a lumberjack and mother a princess from some long-ago kingdom by the sea.

It seemed like there were closets everywhere filled with lots of great stuff. I found my black sneakers, my first baseball glove, a bamboo fishing pole, boxes of old comics, and lots more. When I begged Mom to let me sort through everything, she told me, "No. As soon as I let you look through them, you'll want to keep them all."

"Ah, Mom."

"No!"

"Hey, wait! Look!" At the back of the closet, wedged behind the comics, was a top, a toy top that I knew right away I wanted more than any of the other things.

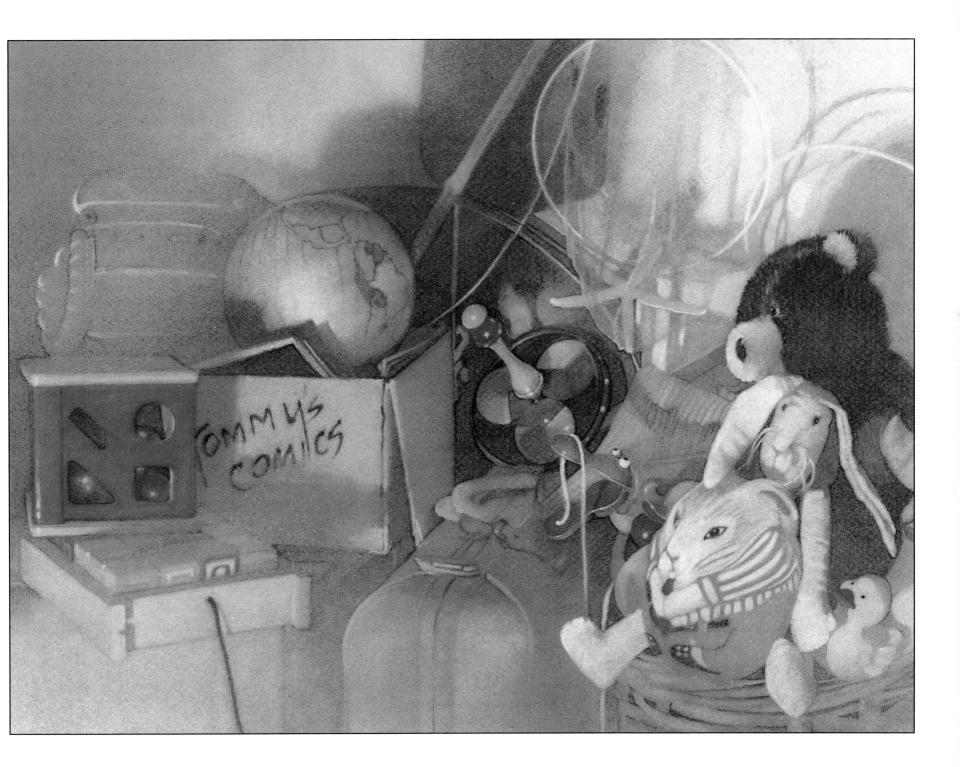

When I saw it, when I picked it up and when I set it down and plunged the plunger down and watched as it spun and whirred and finally wobbled and stopped—I had to have it. Suddenly, I could remember the smell of sawdust, Dad running his power saw, fixing things long ago. And then it hit me. I was moving away, away from this place that had been home ever since I was little playing with this top.

On the following day Dad finished packing up the shed. When he had loaded the last things into the moving trailer, he showed me a wooden box.

"Old horse and buggy tools of my Uncle Jack . . . not much good to anyone now."

"Why you keeping them, then?"

"I guess because they help me remember what he was like and what his times were like, too. I pick these up and I can see him and his team of black mares plain as day. I can even smell Aunt Alice's kitchen filled with fresh baked bread and see her cellar lined with jars of tomatoes glowing like small lanterns on the musty shelves."

I told Dad then about the top I had found and how I wanted it. He understood.

The next day Mom was upstairs in her sewing room and needed help moving a box of patterns. As we dragged it along the floor, I noticed light coming from where the box had stood.

"I thought this was the back of the closet?"

"Not quite. There's a little space there that runs out over the kitchen."

"Can I go back there?"

"Well . . ."

I could see her worrying about a nail or something but she surprised me and said, "OK. Who knows, maybe your father slid something in there."

With a flashlight I could see that just beyond where the pattern box had been wedged, the closet shrunk to half its size and turned. As I scooted forward, knocking down cobwebs, I could see wires, scraps of paper, and a wasp nest. I knew now where our house wasps had come from. About halfway I could see a few more wasps, but nothing else.

I twisted around to start back. As I did, my knee bumped a small box. When I got out with it, I could see that it was a cigar box.

"Why, Tommy, I don't think that's ours. Must be real old. Look."

And there, under the lid, were old letters, clippings, photos, medals from something called the Farmer's Agricultural Show—Moorfield County, 1909. The stuff was ancient, back before there were cars or electricity or anything hardly. Dad told me that it really wasn't ancient but was interesting and must have belonged to a family who lived here long before we did. He said we ought to give it to the Historical Society. But for tonight he told me I could look through it on my own.

I dreamed that night I was riding a horse back from the fair with a
blue ribbon hung around its neck.

Then in the dream the horse was gone. I was lost and no one at the
fair knew who I was.

The next day our moving began to look more serious. The porch was full of boxes and furniture. Mom and Dad told me they were going to take their bed apart next.

"Where are you going to sleep?" I asked.

"On the floor—we'll just use our sleeping bags."

"Me, too! It would be fun."

"What did I tell you," Dad said to Mom, winking his eye.

Great, I thought, camping indoors!

We started with their bed. The big mattress and then the heavy springs were lifted out and leaned against the wall. And then, just like that, a bump here, a knock with the hammer, and there it stood—just the head, the foot, and a pile of boards. I carried the boards, while Mom and Dad tugged and twisted at the mattress and then the springs and slid them all slowly down the stairs and onto the porch. All the other bedroom furniture had been moved to the porch earlier. When I went back up and stomped across the floor, the only thing in it was the loud echoing of my banging feet.

Soon my room was empty, too. Later, as I lay on the floor, I imagined the way it had looked before—my old bed in that corner under the football poster, my chest of drawers, the small desk where I drew cartoons, the bench my mom says was hers when she was little. I wondered if I'd be able to set up my new room just the way this one had been. Then I looked out the window. The idea that the big tree and the garden and the Tolson house across the way with Jimmy in it, that I wouldn't see these anymore, made me wish again we weren't moving. I remembered that dream where no one knew me. My stomach hurt and I had to fight the tears out of my eyes.

The following day was our last full one. I'm glad it was busy since I was feeling more and more the sadness of leaving. We stuffed the trunk of the car with small things: lamps, silverware, blankets, rugs, boots, and one box of toys. No one said anything about my keeping the old top. And I didn't tell where I'd packed the snake's skin!

After supper we sat out on the porch among all the boxes and furniture, the three of us on the old sofa, me in the middle, all watching the sun go down and talking about the things we would remember.

"I'll always remember the wreck this house was at first and how good I felt in making it look nice," Mom said.

"I'll sure miss the woods, all the birds and all the other wildlife,"— that's Dad.

But for me, I couldn't say what it was. It seemed too much. It didn't feel like one thing, but like everything I'd be missing. I wasn't sure if it was better or worse that Mom and Dad were feeling sad. I dreamed that night that I was in our new home and looking out the windows I could still see Jimmy's house and our garden and Mom and Dad walking up the lane. But then the stupid fair where no one knew me showed up across the street. Mom was shaking me awake before I knew anymore.

Roger was first the next day in his blue pickup. Then came Jimmy and his dad, and then Mr. Gorby, and before long there was a fleet of pickups out front and a whole gang of neighbors and friends crowding the house and yard. Some were hand-trucking the refrigerator out the back, while others were sweeping floors and scouring sinks and the bathtub or setting up the plank table for the picnic lunch.

It was hot, hard work. I was proud when Dad hollered for me to help the men who were grunting and sweating as they worked the piano out of the living room and down the steep porch steps.

When Mom finally called us to eat, I remembered that I had wanted to leave something as good luck for the next people. I liked what Mr. Gorby had told me a few nights earlier that leaving a new broom was considered a friendly sort of thing to do. "A new broom sweeps clean." I grabbed the one Mom had just gotten and ran upstairs with it and left it in the middle of my empty room.

I looked out the window. I could see everyone lining up at the table under the pine trees. What a crowd. It was good to know we had so many friends. And, you know, every one of them wished us luck.

As we pulled out the lane, Jimmy was standing across the road waving good-bye. He had promised to write me real soon and I had promised the same. I waved back.

In the car later Mom talked about how we were bringing a lot of the old home with us, not just the things of it, but the memories of it, too. Dad told me I could fill up our new house with memories and in no time at all it would feel good like the old home did. "The best of the old and the best of the new," he said.

Then I told them about the dream and about how worried and sad I was.

"But you'd better leave room to be happy, too."

"Why?"

"Well . . . because there might be some surprises, too."

"Like what?!"

"It wouldn't be a surprise if we told you."

They were right, it wouldn't. But I'll tell you this. Some surprises were cold and sweet. Some were round, bright, and floated all around us. And some were words in a letter mailed by a Jimmy that was sooner than "soon."

That first night in my new room, in my old bed, I dreamed about the fair. But this time I knew the people and they had voices that said "hello" and "welcome" and "glad to meet you."

*For all the good people from Sand Hill to Moundsville, from Bowman Ridge to St. Joseph's, and places between and beyond, friends and neighbors.*
*M.H.*

*To Zoë, who has waited and played so patiently under my desk for nearly a year.*
*W.P.*

Library of Congress Cataloging-in-Publication Data
Harshman, Marc.  Moving days / Marc Harshman ; illustrated by Wendy Popp.  p.     cm.
Summary: As he and his parents prepare to move from the country to the city, a boy shares memories
about the old house they are leaving and his worries about their new home.
ISBN 0-525-65135-7
[1. Moving, Household—Fiction.  2. Parent and child—Fiction.]  I. Popp, Wendy, ill.  II. Title.
H256247Mo  1994  [E]—dc20  92-31901  CIP  AC
Published in the United States by Cobblehill Books, an affiliate of Dutton Children's Books,
a division of Penguin Books USA Inc., 375 Hudson Street, New York, New York 10014
Designed by Kathleen Westray  Printed in Hong Kong  First Edition
10  9  8  7  6  5  4  3  2  1